This book belongs to

The Adventures of

Bella & Harry

Let's Visit Venice!

Written By

Lisa Manzione

Illustrated By

Kristine Lucco

Bella & Harry, LLC

www.BellaAndHarry.com
email: BellaAndHarryGo@aol.com

Hi! It's me, Bella. Harry is here too! We are off to Venice, Italy with our family.

Italy is located in Europe.

"Harry, did you know Europe is the sixth largest continent in the world? A continent is a large piece of land, usually surrounded by water. There are seven continents in the world."

VENICE

I have a great idea! Let's look at a picture of Italy together on the map. Our boy says Italy looks like a boot. Do you think Italy looks like a boot? I do! It looks like Venice is located at the top of the boot.

Let's go. It is time to get started on our tour of the city.

"Bella...

where are all the cars?"

"Well Harry, there are no cars in Venice."

"No cars? How do Chihuahuas like us get around?"

"There are a few ways to travel in the city of Venice. We can walk through the small, winding streets, or we can ride through the canals. Canals are streets made of water. If we travel through the canals, we must ride in a small boat to get from place to place."

10

"Ride in a boat, Bella?"

"Yes, the boats are known as gondolas. I think our children will take us for a ride later. Harry, be careful when you are near the water or riding in the gondola. If you lean over the edge, you might fall in the water!"

"Okay, Bella. I will be very careful when I am near the water or riding in the gondola."

13

"We are off to the Piazza St. Marco. It is also called St. Mark's Square. It was the main meeting place hundreds of years ago for the local people and still is a very popular meeting place today. This meeting place is a big open area where people and puppies meet to have fun!"

"Look, Harry! There are pigeons everywhere!"

14

"Bella, let's chase the pigeons!"

"Harry, come back here! Harry!"

15

Suddenly, Harry stopped

running and started staring at the sky.

"What do you see, Harry?"

"Look over there Bella. I see a lion
in the sky.. and it has wings!"

"Harry, that is not just any lion. The lion
is the symbol of St. Mark, the patron saint of Venice."

"Bella, what is a patron saint?"

"A patron saint is
someone who watches
over someone or
something, and in this
instance, protects the
city. Just as our family
watches and protects us!"

16

"Wow!
That's a very
important job!"

"Bella, I'm tired."

"Harry, we are stopping for lunch with our family now."

"Bella, what's on the menu?"

"Hmm... well, it looks like pizza."

"Bella, what is pizza?"

"**Pizza** is flat bread, usually with toppings, such as cheese or tomatoes. The first modern pizza in Italy was probably created for Queen Margherita. It was made with cheese, tomatoes and basil. The colors of the first pizza match the Italian flag; red, white and green!"

"Yummy!"

"Harry... you are a Chihuahua. You don't eat pizza!"

"Oh, yeah... I forgot."

Well, now that we have rested we're off again to the Rialto Bridge.

"Wow! Harry, look at the cool bridge! Did you know this bridge was built more than four hundred years ago? The bridge is about 15 feet long, about 6 full size elephants standing in a line, and about 7 feet wide, which is about one elephant... sideways."

"**Bella,** let's race over the bridge.
Last Chihuahua over the bridge is a... CAT!"

21

"**Yay!** I won!"

"Yes, Harry, you won! You are a very fast Chihuahua."

22

"Bella, here is your cat mask!"

"Harry, where did you find such a perfect mask?"

"I found the cat mask in a gift shop, next to the Rialto Bridge."

23

Masks are very common in Venice. The masks are referred to as Venetian masks. The masks are very popular souvenirs of this wonderful city. Each year there is a carnival here during the month of February or March. It is called the "Carnevale di Venezia".

"Bella, that sounds like a lot of fun! Maybe we can come back to Venice to see the carnival."

"We might return to Venice later, but now I think it is time for our gondola ride.   Come on Harry... let's go!"

"Bella, this is the neatest thing we've ever done! Riding in a boat pushed by a pole!"

Suddenly Bella lost her balance
and fell out of the gondola!

"Bella! Bella!! Swim! Swim... with all four paws!"

"**Oh,** Bella! How scary! *You* fell out of the gondola, not me!"

"Yes, Harry, I fell out of the gondola. I should have been more careful. Even big sisters have accidents. I am so happy you were there to help me."

29

"Bella, we are stopping for a snack. I think the children are having ice cream."

"Actually, Harry, it is called 'gelato'. Gelato is the Italian word for ice cream. Gelato is different than ice cream because it has more whole milk. It is stirred at a slower speed than ice cream, and frozen at a warmer temperature, so the gelato is much softer to eat than ice cream."

"Yummmmy!"

"Don't forget Harry, you don't eat gelato either! You are a puppy...
a very silly puppy!"

"Yes, and a puppy that loves gelato!"

Well, our tour of Venice is over for now. I think our family is planning another exciting adventure. Harry and I would really like you to join us. We'll have a great time! But for now... "arrivederci", or good-bye, from Bella Boo and Harry too!

Our Adventure to Venice

A fun ride!

Bella... ready for the carnival!

Harry... enjoying a bowl of spaghetti
and meatballs! Yummy!

Fast Friends!

33

Exploring Venice!

A friendly pigeon from St. Mark's Square.

Relaxing after a long day.

A beautiful Venetian sunset.

Fun Italian Phrases and Words...

Ciao! or Pronto! - Hello!

Arrivederci - Good-bye

Grazie - Thank you

Prego or Per favore - Please

Cane - Dog

Cane di Piccola Taglia - Small dog

Parli Italiano? - Do you speak Italian?

Io non parlo Italiano. - I do not speak Italian.

Amo la mia famiglia. - I love my family.

Library of Congress Cataloging-in-Publications Data is available

Manzione, Lisa

The Adventures of Bella & Harry: Let's Visit Venice!

ISBN: 978-1-937616-02-1

Second Edition

Book Two of Bella & Harry Series

For further information please visit:

www.BellaAndHarry.com

or

Email: BellaAndHarryGo@aol.com

CPSIA Section 103 (a) Compliant

www.beaconstar.com/ consumer

ID: L0118329. Tracking No.: L1312347-7926

Printed in China